A Note to Parents & Caregivers—

Reading Stars books are designed to build confidence in the earliest of readers. Relying on word repetition and visual cues, each book features fewer than 50 words.

You can help your child develop a lifetime love of reading right from the very start. Here are some ways to help your beginning reader get going:

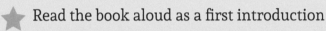 Read the book aloud as a first introduction

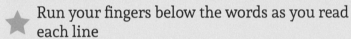 Run your fingers below the words as you read each line

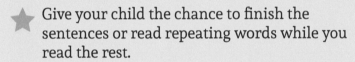 Give your child the chance to finish the sentences or read repeating words while you read the rest.

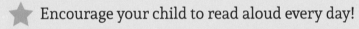 Encourage your child to read aloud every day!

Every Child can be a Reading Star!

Published in the United States by Xist Publishing
www.xistpublishing.com

First Edition
eISBN: 978-1-5324-1603-3
Paperback ISBN: 978-1-5324-1604-0
Hardcover ISBN: 978-1-5324-1605-7
Printed in the United States of America

This Day

Juliana O'Neill
Ding LinHui

x*ist Publishing

It is time to play.

This will be a good day.

This day will have fun.

This day will have sun.

This day will have walks.

This day will have talks.

16

What makes a
good day?

A day filled with play!

This day is done.

20

It was a good one.

I am a Reading Star
because I can read the
words in this book:

a	sun
be	talks
day	this
done	time
filled	to
fun	walks
good	was
have	what
is	will
It	with
makes	
one	
play	

xist Publishing

CPSIA information can be obtained
at www.ICGtesting.com
Printed in the USA
LVHW070108061221
705384LV00005B/118

9 781532 416057